Princess Madison
and the Whispering Woods

KAREN SCALF LINAMEN
ILLUSTRATED BY PHYLLIS HORNUNG

Revell
Grand Rapids, Michigan

Text © 2006 by Karen Scalf Linamen
Illustrations © 2006 by Phyllis Hornung

Published by Fleming H. Revell
a division of Baker Publishing Group
P.O. Box 6287, Grand Rapids, MI 49516-6287
www.revellbooks.com

Printed in the United States of America

Library of Congress Cataloging-in-Publication Data
Linamen, Karen Scalf, 1960–
   Princess Madison and the Whispering Woods / Karen Scalf Linamen ; illustrated by Phyllis Hornung.
      p.   cm. — (Princess Madison ; bk. 2)
   Summary: Sad because her father is going on a business trip, Madison leaves the castle and, although she knows she should not, enters the woods, gets lost, and stays out after dark, but what she fears most is that her father cannot love her after her misdeeds.
   ISBN 10: 0-8007-1842-9 (cloth)
   ISBN 978-0-8007-1842-8 (cloth)
   [1. Fathers and daughters—Fiction. 2. Love—Fiction. 3. Lost children—Fiction. 4. Princesses—Fiction.]
I. Hornung, Phyllis, ill. II. Title. III. Series: Linamen, Karen Scalf, 1960– Princess Madison ; bk. 2.
PZ7.L6467Prj 2006
[E]—dc22   2006011751

For Mom and Dad,

who have rescued me from

many a scary place

madison's father was going on a business trip.

Madison helped him polish his crown. She helped him pack his socks. She even carried one of his bags all the way to the limo.

When she hugged him good-bye, Madison asked him a question. It was the same question she asked him every night at bedtime. She said, "Daddy, how much do you love me?"

Her father laughed and gave her the same answer he had given her the night before and all the nights before that.

He said, "My love for you is bigger than all the mountains in all the countries in all the world. It's greater than all the grains of sand at the bottom of all the oceans over all the earth. And it's brighter than the sun, the moon, and all the stars in the sky."

As the limo drove away, Madison smelled something wonderful—chocolate chip cookies. In the kitchen, she saw Cook pouring something into a spoon and then into a mixing bowl.

"What are you doing?" Madison asked.

"Measuring salt," said Cook.

"Why did you pour it in the spoon first?" Madison asked.

"Because a pinch of prevention is better than a cup of cure," said Cook.

"I thought you said it was salt."

Cook laughed. "Prevention means being careful. Cure means fixing things when you're not careful."

Madison thought about that. "So . . . a bit of careful is better than a lot of fixing?"

"Yup," said Cook.

Madison said, "I'm going outside to play."

"Stay out of the forest and be home before dark!" Cook warned.

"Don't worry," Madison said. "I'll be home soon for cookies."

adison headed for the archery range. This is where all the king's horses and all the king's men practiced shooting arrows at targets just in case they ever landed a guest spot on the David Letterman show. Madison wanted to shoot an arrow too.

Bill, the archery master, said, "No way. Not today. When you're older I'll teach you how to use a bow and arrow. Until then you'd better play somewhere else."

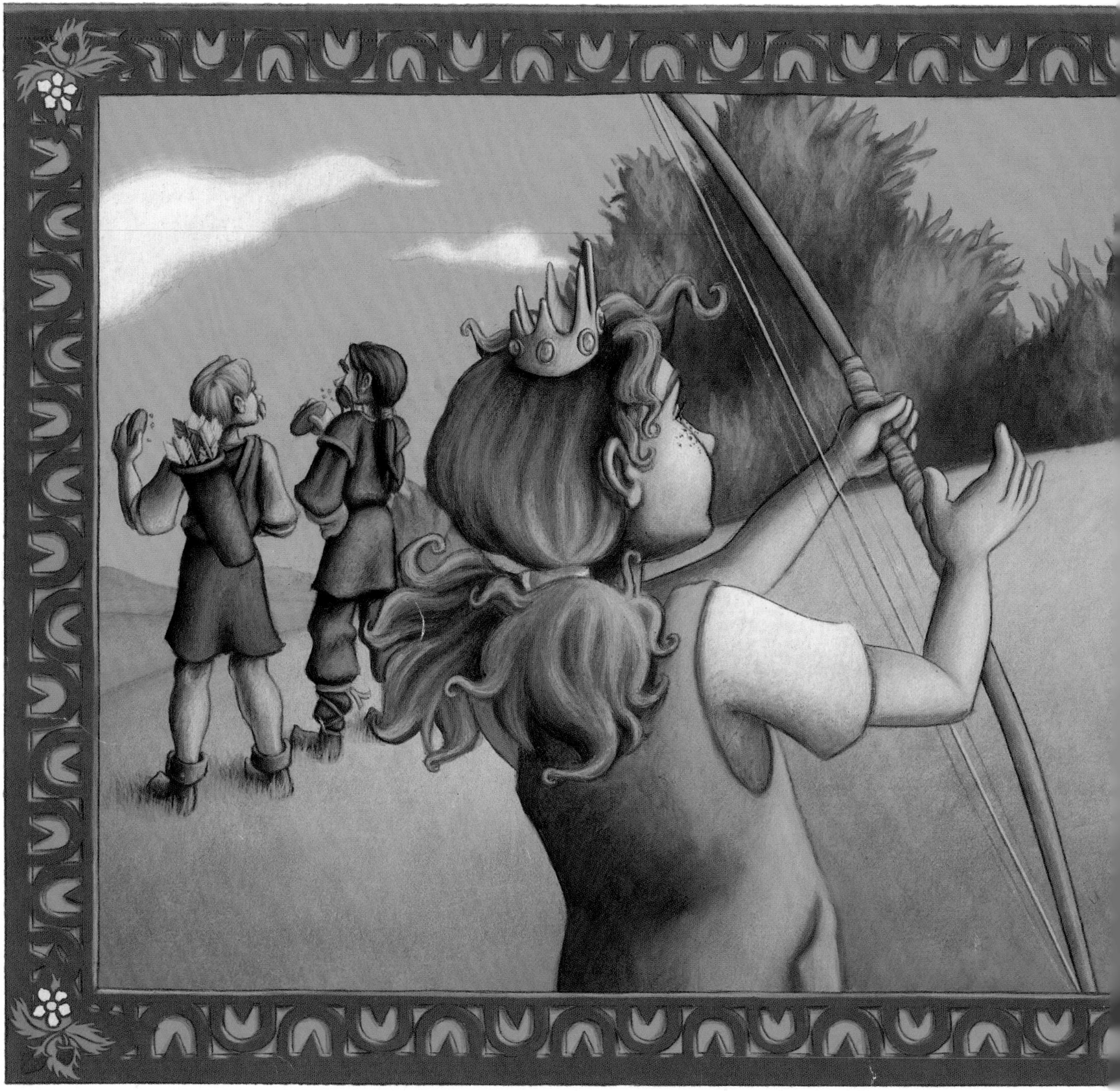

When no one was looking, Madison grabbed an arrow. She fit it into the bow and pulled hard.

The arrow didn't fly toward the heart of the target like Madison had imagined. Instead, it flew straight into the forest.

This was *not* a good thing.

*J*ust inside the forest grew a patch of thorny brambles. Inside the brambles was an anthill. Sticking out of the anthill was the arrow.

"Ouch!" Madison said as she wriggled past the thorns. When she pulled the arrow from the anthill, she saw the tip was broken.

This was *really* not a good thing.

Madison sat down. Her arms and legs stung from the thorns. Her heart felt heavy. Watching the ants, she told them, "I wasn't supposed to shoot an arrow, and now it's broken. My father told me his love for me was as big as a mountain. I bet when he sees what I've done, his love for me will be the size of your little anthill instead."

The ants were silent, so Madison watched two butterflies. When they flew deeper into the forest, Madison jumped to her feet.

She said, "Those cookies have probably all been eaten by now anyway. I'll see where those butterflies live, and *then* I'll go home."

The ants waved at Madison. She thought they were saying, "Good-bye and good luck," but it's possible they were saying, "Wait! Stop! Don't go into those woods!" Yes, quite possible indeed.

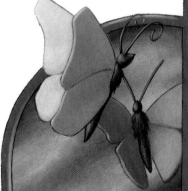

madison followed the butterflies past a chattering brook. Past a meadow. Past the secret den of a hungry fox who watched Madison with piercing yellow eyes.

Her stomach growled. She thought of the cookies, and her stomach growled more. She wanted to go home, except she wasn't sure how to get there anymore.

She passed a mossy boulder. She traveled through a patch of ferns with fragile fingers that brushed her legs. She crossed the shadowy entrance of a musty cave and thought of bears and dragons and cookies.

Searching her pockets, she found only a few crumbs from a Rice Krispies Treat.

This was really, *really* not a good thing.

She said to the butterflies, "I wasn't supposed to go into the woods, and now I'm lost. My father told me his love for me was as much as all the grains of sand in all the oceans over all the earth. I bet when he finds out what I've done, his love for me will be about the size of these Rice Krispies grains instead."

Madison ate the crumbs and wondered how she was going to find her way home.

The colors of the day began to fade. The leaves in the trees began to look dark and gray. The forest shadows—so cool and inviting when the day was warm—began to stretch and grow into dark hungry shapes that before very long at all had gobbled up most of the forest.

This was really, really, *really* not a good thing.

Madison wondered what shadows liked to eat for dessert and hoped it wasn't princess à la mode.

madison thought of home. Was Cook watching reality shows on TV? Was Madison's sister Evangeline on the phone again? Was Mother at her dressing table, taking off her crown and brushing her hair before bed? Was anyone worried about Madison? Had anyone noticed she was gone?

A fragile wink of light caught Madison's attention, and a firefly landed on her finger. Madison said sadly to the little bug, "I wasn't supposed to stay out after dark, and now I'm lost and scared. My father told me his love for me was as bright as the sun and moon and all the stars. I bet when he hears about what I've done, his love for me won't be any brighter than you are right now."

She began to cry.

Suddenly Madison heard something crashing through the woods.

It was crashing loudly and crashing fast, and whatever it was, it was

crashing

right

toward

her!

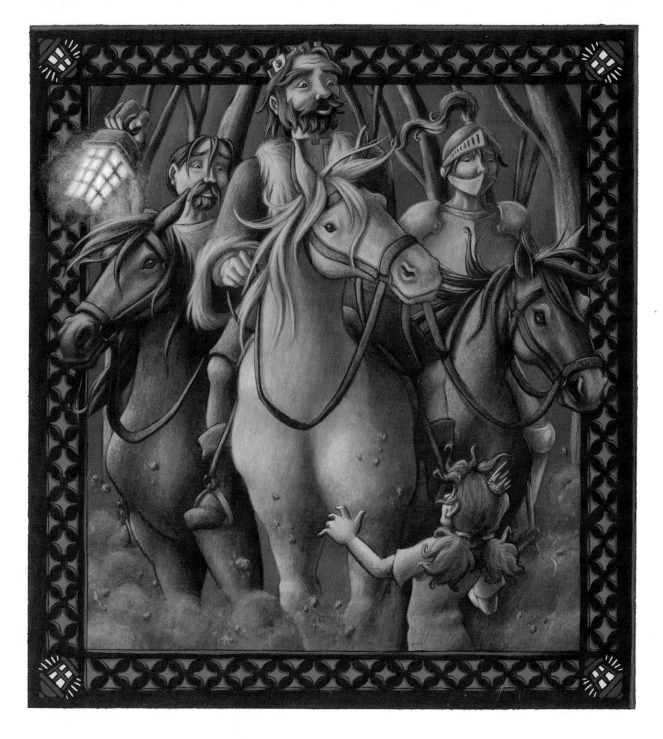

In an instant the woods and the dark gave way to chaos and voices and light.

Three huge beasts were upon Madison, shaking and jingling and blowing. Upon the beasts sat three men: Madison's father, Bill the archery master, and Sir Ohmygoodness, one of the king's bravest knights.

Madison's father wrapped her in a blanket. He put Band-Aids on her scratches. He gave her Kleenex for her runny nose. He gave her water and Pop-Tarts and as many cheese sticks as she wanted.

In the meantime, Sir Ohmygoodness stood guard in case the fox with the piercing yellow eyes or the bear from the musty cave decided to join their party, and Bill called the queen on his cell phone to let her know that Madison had been found.

The horses carried Madison and her three rescuers back past the shadowy entrance of the musty cave,

. . . past the patch of ferns with fragile fingers,

. . . past the mossy boulder,

. . . past the secret den of the hungry fox,

. . . past the meadow and chattering brook,

. . . through the thorny brambles,

. . . beyond the archery range,

. . . right to the front yard of the castle, where Madison's mom, Madison's sister, the Cook, the castle doctor, a reporter for the castle newspaper, and a dozen other people were waiting anxiously for Madison to come home.

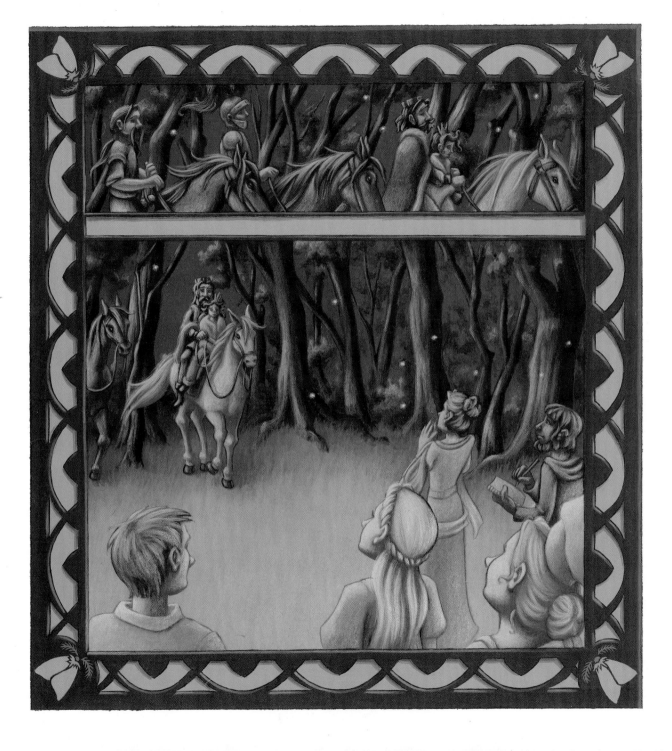

madison got long hugs, a long bath, and an even longer lecture. She had to swallow a spoonful of cold medicine that tasted kind of like dirt.

$m$adison finally got to eat some cookies. She got new Band-Aids after her bath too. Her mother kissed her good night just like always.

Her father kissed her good night just like always.

Her parents waited, but Madison didn't ask the bedtime question she had asked every night for a very, very long time.

Her father said, "Did you forget something?"

She said, "No."

He said, "Don't you want to know how much I love you?"

She said, "I think I know."

He said, "You do?"

Madison said, "Your love for me is the same size as a little anthill. It's no greater than a few grains of a Rice Krispies Treat. And it's about as bright as a firefly."

He said, "Why would you think that?"

She said, "I should have been more careful and used a pinch of prevention. I didn't follow the rules, and I needed a *whole bunch* of fixing instead!"